Susan Amundson
Nan Holt

nawk

In memory of Millie who kept a special place in her heart for animals.
– S.A.

Thank you to Greg and Lori Sorenson for permission to use Legend's name in this story, to Betty Gerlach for using her kennel name Snowberry and to Brenda Geiken for assignment of copyright to use her cover art of *A Child's Happy Heart* and *Free To Be Me The Eskimo Way* in this story.

Bjelkiersam HERO ® is a trademark of Susan Amundson
Text © 2012 by Susan Amundson
Illustration © 2012 by Nan Holt
Book design by Graphic Design, Inc., Hastings, MN
Edited by Mary Jo Tate
Bjelkier Press
1620 Louis Lane
Hastings, MN  55033
Printed in the United States of America

**Visit us at www.toysammy.com**

**Publisher's Cataloging-in-Publication**

    Amundson, Susan D.
      Hero finds his path / by Susan Amundson;
  illustrator, Nan Holt.
    p. cm.
      SUMMARY: Hero, a young Samoyed show dog, wants to be
  a champion like his daddy. But when he is rejected, he
  learns to deal with this challenge by finding another
  path.
    Audience: Ages 3-7.
    ISBN-13: 978-0-9828217-4-9
    ISBN-10: 0-9828217-4-3

    1. Samoyed dog--Juvenile fiction.  2. Rejection
(Psychology)--Juvenile fiction.  3. Fathers and sons--
Juvenile fiction.  [1. Dogs--Fiction.  2. Samoyed dog--
Fiction.  3. Rejection (Psychology)--Fiction.
4. Fathers and sons--Fiction.]  I. Holt, Nan, ill.  II. Title.

  PZ7.A518216Her 2012      [E]
        QBI10-600153

Library of Congress Control Number: 2011912861

First Edition
The text of this book is set in Berkeley Oldstyle Medium.
The illustrations are rendered in color pencil and watercolor crayon on multimedia board.

CPSIA facility code: BP 313741

# Hero Finds His Path

## Susan Amundson
*Illustrated by **Nan Holt***

*Bjelkier Press*
Hastings, Minnesota

Hi! My name is Hero.

I'm a cute and fluffy
Samoyed puppy.

Dog shows are fun.
Everyone there
loves me.

The judges
like me too.

I know I'll be a champion someday.

I trot around the show ring.

I raise my head up high, up to the sky, and show off my stuff.

A treat smells good and helps me stand perfectly.

I eat it. Yum!

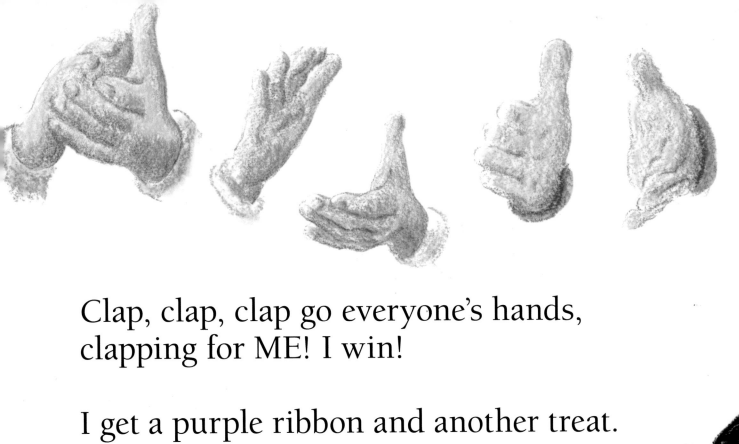

Clap, clap, clap go everyone's hands, clapping for ME! I win!

I get a purple ribbon and another treat.

Someday I'll be a champion like
my daddy, Legend.  I'm sure I will.

Everyone says I look like him.

He can even pull sleds.

THEN
SOMETHING
AWFUL
HAPPENS…

I stop winning.

They say I'm not big enough
        to be a champ.

Those judges like my daddy
but not me.

IF THEY DON'T LIKE ME,
I DON'T LIKE ME.

Crying doesn't fix my problem.

Pouting doesn't help either.

I grow, but not as big as a show champ.
I'm still cute and lovable.

People see me having fun, running,
and playing.

They like me…everything about me!

One day I see toys that look like me.
Then I see puppets that look like me.

In Khobi and Hero books,
the Samoyed looks like me.

It IS me!

My name is everywhere too!

It's on those toys, puppets, and books.

I fly in planes

and ride in cars to visit children at schools,
libraries, and bookstores.

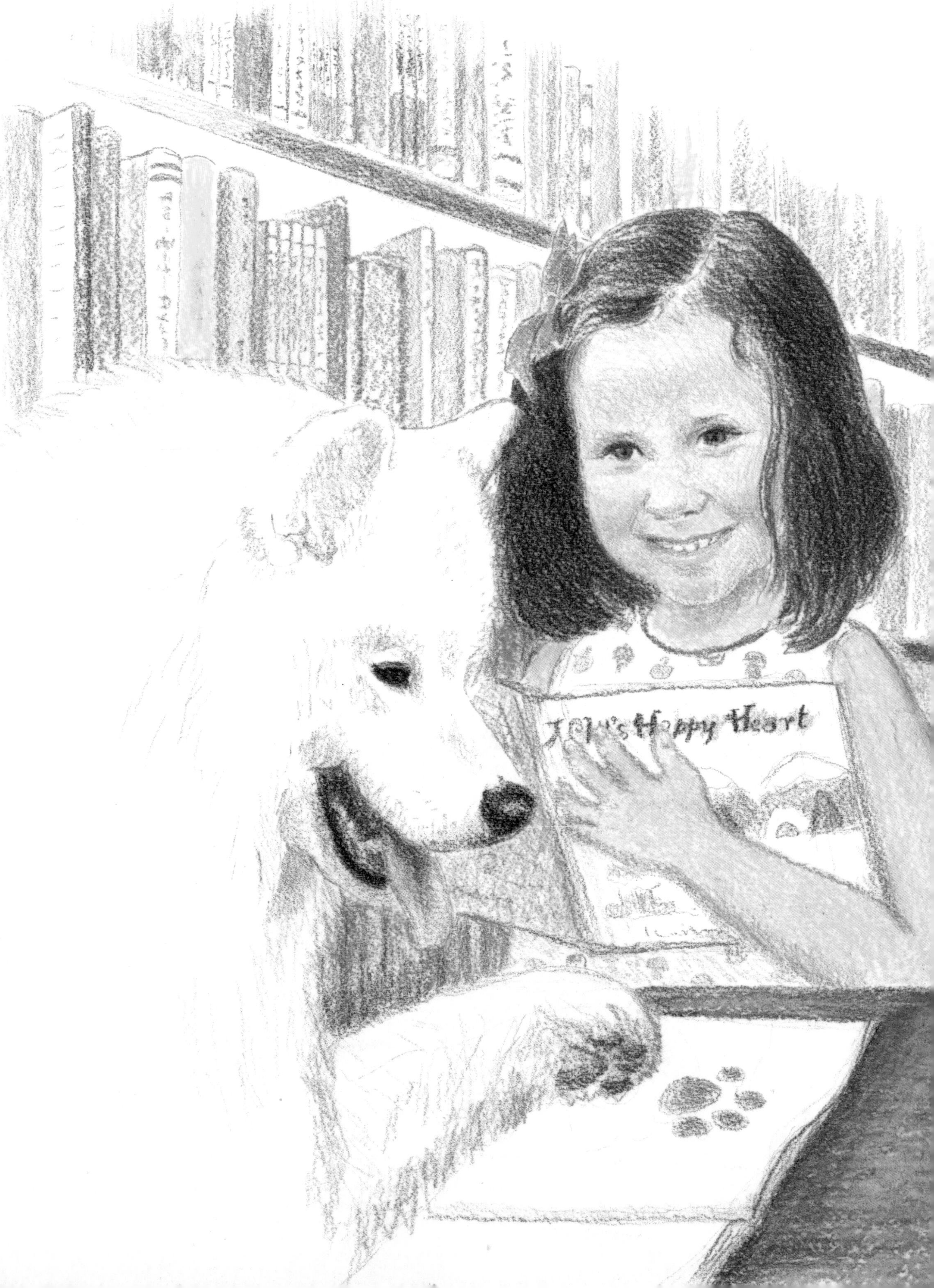
Happy Heart

I make them smile when
I sign Khobi and Hero books
with my paw.

Everyone loves me.
Even grown-ups love me.

I give them sloppy doggy kisses.

My tail swishes fast
because I'm happy.

I hold my head up
    high again because . . .

I found what I do best and

I LIKE WHO I AM!

# Author Notes

HERO FINDS HIS PATH is a true story about my Samoyed, Snowberry's Legendary Hero. My wish in sharing Hero's story is that children will know there is a place for them in this big world. No matter who you are or what you are, something good is waiting for you even if it turns out to be plan "B". Hero visited children in schools. Seeing how children loved Hero inspired me to write children's books.

My other published titles are: *A Child's Happy Heart*, a Midwest Book Review "thumbs up". It has stood the test of time and has now been transitioned into a classroom play by playwright Diane Purdy titled *A Happy Heart Heals. Free To Be Me The Eskimo Way, Mikey Makes The Team*, and *Three Little Lambs…Somewhere* also a Midwest Book Review "thumbs up" complete the list.

I live in Minnesota with my husband and beautiful Tabby, a Samoyed. We have three grown children and two grandchildren.

# About the Illustrator

I have drawn and painted animals as long as I can remember. Sometime in the early 80's, I made a connection with the dog show world, and Dog Art was born. Over the years, I have provided logo paintings, awards, and trophies for many clubs, painting their breeds on all kinds of surfaces.

Samoyed Fanciers have been among my most loyal customers. The warm reception my work has received at the specialties has inspired much creativity.

Illustrating Hero Finds his Path has been a joy. It is my hope that my paintings have brought Susan's wonderful story to life.

I live and work in rural Virginia with my husband, Phil and my silky terrier, Halle. We have two grown sons and three grandchildren.

# A LITTLE MORE ABOUT SAMOYEDS

The Samoyed is a highly intelligent breed whose thinking is similar to humans. They are known as the "Christmas Dog" who smiles all year long.

Beautiful and stunning, this medium-sized sled dog is double coated to survive the brutal Arctic climate. Their temperament is gentle with a special connection to children.

This working breed stands 19 to 23 ½ inches at the shoulders and weighs somewhere between 45 and 65 pounds.

Sa-moid' is a common pronunciation, although there are different ones. Because of that many people refer to the breed as Sam.